SAM SILVER: UNDERCOVER PIRATE

SKELETON
ISLAND

Collect all the Sam Silver: Undercover Pirate *books*

SKELETON ISLAND

Jan Burchett and Sara Vogler

Illustrated by Leo Hartas

Orion
Children's Books

First published in Great Britain in 2012
by Orion Children's Books
a division of the Orion Publishing Group Ltd
Orion House
5 Upper St Martin's Lane
London WC2H 9EA
An Hachette UK company

1 3 5 7 9 10 8 6 4 2

Text copyright © Jan Burchett and Sara Vogler 2012
Map and interior illustrations copyright © Leo Hartas 2012

A catalogue record for this book is
available from the British Library.

ISBN 978 1 4440 0584 4

Printed in Great Britain by Clays Ltd, St Ives plc

For Thomas Vogler.
With love from your mothers.

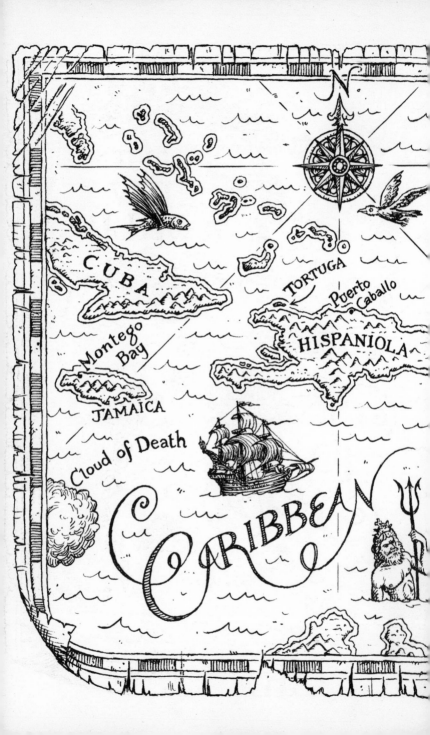

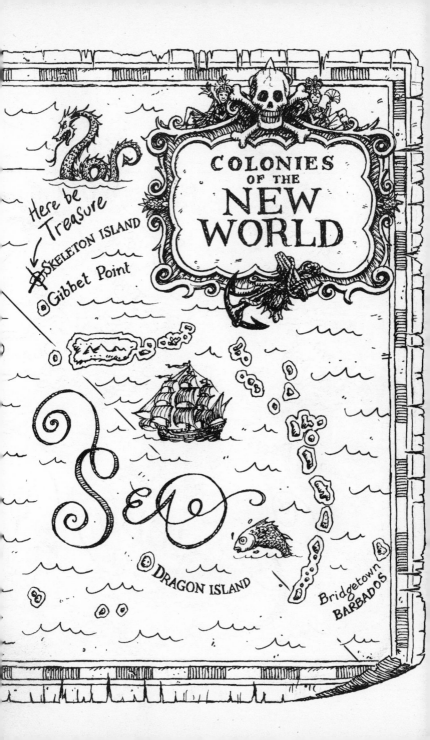

COLONIES
OF THE
NEW
WORLD

Here be Treasure
SKELETON ISLAND
Gibbet Point

Sea

DRAGON ISLAND

Bridgetown
BARBADOS

The SEA WOLF

Captain's Cabin

Hammocks

Gun Deck

Galley

Ship's Stores

CHAPTER ONE

Sam Silver raced across the empty
beach, football at his feet. He
dodged a pile of seaweed, swerved
round a sandcastle and blasted the ball
at the cliff.

"Goal!" he shouted. "Sam Silver wins
the World Cup – again!"

He ran through the waves, saluting his
imaginary fans. *Clunk!* His foot caught

on something
hard, sending
him sprawling in the
foam.

A bottle was bobbing
in the surf. As Sam scrambled
to his feet it rolled back towards
him, spun a couple of times and lodged
itself between his trainers. He pushed
his wet hair out of his eyes and picked it
up. It was green and sand-pitted with a
blackened cork.

"Cool!" he said. "I've never seen a bottle
like this. It's perfect for my collection."

Sam's treasure collection was the best
in Backwater Bay — at least he thought
so. His bedroom shelf was heaving with
wonderful finds from the beach. He had
a razor shell as long as his arm, a gnarly
stone that could be a sailor's finger bone,
and a gold ring that must have come from
some sunken Viking hoard. His most

prized possession was a pirate's peg leg.
Dad said it was probably from an old table
dumped in the sea, but Sam knew it had
belonged to a swashbuckling buccaneer.

He shook the bottle. Something was in
there.

"That'll be a message from a castaway!"
exclaimed Sam.

The cork was stuck fast. There was
only one thing for it. He'd dash home,
force the cork out, read the message
and phone the coastguard to rescue the
stranded sailor.

He bounded up the stone steps to
the high street and sprinted along to
his parents' shop – The Jolly Cod,
Best Fish and Chips in Backwater Bay.
The warm smell of cooking oil wafted
into the street as he flung open the
door.

Ducking under the hatch in the counter
he came face to face with a tray of fish

fillets. His mum was glaring down at him over the top.

"Why are you soaking wet?" she demanded. "And what's that? Not another find for your collection."

"It's a bottle with a message from a castaway on a desert island," Sam panted. "He needs rescuing."

"No one sends messages in bottles any more," said his mum, grinning. "Now get out of those wet jeans and T-shirt."

Sam sped upstairs. He didn't have time to change. Every second counted. He prodded the cork with a paperclip but the cork didn't move. He tried levering it out with a pencil but the lead snapped.

He needed something stronger. He found his mum's metal nail file and dug the pointed end into the cork, twisting with all his strength.

Pop! The cork flew out. Sam knew his mum wouldn't be pleased about her nail file, which was now bent, but she'd forget about it when he was on the cover of the *Backwater Bay Gazette* for saving someone's life. And his friends would be dead impressed.

He stuck his finger into the bottle neck. A thin scroll of crinkly brown paper appeared. He unrolled it, excitement bubbling in his stomach.
The writing was faint and difficult to make out.

The year of our Lord 1705

"1705!" Sam exclaimed. "That's more than three hundred years ago. It's a bit late for a coastguard rescue."

He read on.

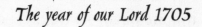

The year of our Lord 1705

I am shipwrecked alone on this island. I will soon be dead of a mortal fever so I must write of what I have found.

Treasure! It is no good to me now but I want my kin, my own family, to have it.

I know not where this cursed island lies. We had sailed two full days east from Tortuga when we were blown well off course by a tempest. We were wrecked on a rock that looked like a giant shark fin rising from the waves.

You will find a gold coin in the bottle. This doubloon is from the treasure and I swear a pirate's oath on it that what I write is true. It will lead you to the riches if you use your wits.

I charge the sea to deliver this letter to my kin and none else.

Joseph Silver, Captain of the Sea Wolf

Sam gawped at the letter. The writer was a real live pirate — well, he'd been alive three centuries ago. And he had the same surname as Sam! Captain Joseph Silver had told the sea to deliver the bottle to a member of his family and it had delivered it to him, Sam Silver.

"I've got pirate blood in my veins!" he gasped in delight. "Avast there, you scurvy knave!" Sam stashed the letter in his pocket and struck a fierce pirate pose at his reflection in the mirror. "No one dares fight Sam Silver, greatest buccaneer that ever lived."

"Sam!" It was his mum from downstairs in the shop. "I need help on the till."

"Coming." Sam made for the door, then stopped. The letter had mentioned a gold doubloon. He shook the bottle and a piece of dirty cloth fell out. Inside was a dull brown coin. It didn't look like gold. He spat on it and gave it a quick rub on his sleeve.

All at once his bedroom walls began to spin! Sam tried to grab hold of his bed

but he was lifted off his feet. His telly and wardrobe were whirling with him. He felt as if he was being sucked up by a giant vacuum cleaner. Sam shut his eyes as he spun round and round.

Suddenly everything stopped and he landed with a bump. He opened his eyes. He was pleased to see that the walls had stopped spinning. Then he realised they weren't his walls. His bedroom had completely disappeared!

CHAPTER TWO

Sam found himself in a small dark room, lit only by a lantern swinging from the ceiling. The air was hot and stifling. There was a thick column like a tree trunk in the centre of the room and coiled ropes everywhere. It looked as if he'd landed in a cupboard – but the floor was rocking!

"Where am I?" he mumbled dizzily.

He stared at the coin in his hand.

Everything had gone weird after he'd given it a rub. He thought about his mum. She'd be wondering why he hadn't come to help her.

The door burst open and a boy strode in. He wore a tattered waistcoat and dirty knee-length trousers and his feet were bare. He was a bit older than Sam with long hair that was wild and curly. A bright bandana kept it out of his eyes. In an instant he'd grabbed Sam and pushed him against the wall, his dark eyes glaring at him suspiciously.

"Who are you?" he growled. He spoke with a foreign accent.

"I'm Sam," said Sam. "You're not going to believe this but I was in my bedroom, Mum was yelling from the fish and chip shop, and my telly and everything started . . ."

"Fish and chip shop? Telly? What mad talk is this?"

"Fernando!" came a shout. "We're waiting for that rope."

"Aye, aye!" the boy called back. He waved a dagger in Sam's face. "You're coming with me. Do not think of escaping for I can throw this blade quicker than you can blink."

He swung a coil of rope on to his shoulder and pushed Sam up a narrow staircase.

Sam stumbled out onto a wooden deck, blinking in the bright sunlight. He could see barrels and rigging and rows of cannon and the deep blue sea beyond. He was on a ship! And one thing was certain. He wasn't in Backwater Bay. The weather was far too hot and there was no land in sight. The ship looked splintered and battered as if it had been in a fight. Men, dressed like the boy behind him, were busy on the long, narrow deck, mending sails, sawing wood and painting things with tar. Three towering masts, their sails billowing, rose above him. A flag fluttered in the wind from the highest mast. It was black, with

 a picture of what looked like a snarling dog's head over a pair of crossed bones.

Sam knew a pirate flag when he saw one!

"Captain Blade!" yelled Fernando, his dagger still pressed into Sam's back. "I found this boy below."

A tall man strode up to them. He wasn't dressed like the others. His long coat had deep cuffs and shiny brass buttons. His hair and beard were braided with threads, and on his finger a ring with a blood red stone glinted fiercely. Leather belts bristling with guns and knives lay diagonally across his chest.

"By the stars, a stowaway!" he declared, his hand on the hilt of a vicious-looking cutlass. His voice was deep and commanding. "How did you slip on board, boy?"

"I have no idea," said Sam, bewildered. "I just found myself in your cupboard.

Hang on, is this a TV programme? Where are the hidden cameras?"

"He keeps gabbling nonsense, Captain," said Fernando, pushing Sam forwards. "He's pretending he doesn't know how he got here but I'm not fooled. His clothes are wet. He swam."

More pirates were gathering round. A short, stout man stomped up, his wooden leg thumping on the deck. He pulled at

Sam's T-shirt with its picture of a Formula One racing car, and peered at his jeans and trainers. "Stap me! They be strange clothes."

"Not as strange as yours!" laughed Sam.

"Maybe he's a spy for the governor," sneered Fernando.

"Or a thief," called a gruff voice.

"Throw him overboard," shouted the short, stout man.

"That's right, Mr Hopp!" said Fernando. The crew pressed forwards. To Sam's horror, he suddenly found himself bundled onto the rail and staring down at the deep water below. This joke wasn't so funny any more.

"Avast!" barked Captain Blade. "We'll hear his story first."

"Aye, Captain," said Harry Hopp, with a nasty grin. "The sharks won't mind waiting."

"Look," said Sam. "I don't know what's going on here. I'm Sam Silver and—"

He was interrupted by a gasp from the crew.

"Set him free!" ordered the captain.

Sam was pulled down onto the deck. Harry Hopp patted him on the back.

"He must be Joseph Silver's kin," someone whispered. "A grandson perhaps."

"Joseph Silver was the finest pirate in the Caribbean," added another. "We can't harm one of his family."

"Why are you here, Sam Silver?" asked the captain.

"I know why the lad's come to us," said Harry Hopp. "Stands to reason. Our ship's named the *Sea Wolf* now we've got Silver's figurehead. We didn't steal it though," he said quickly to Sam. "We found it in the sea after his ship was lost last year."

"Last year?" exclaimed Sam. "Don't you mean three hundred . . ." He stopped. The amazing truth had begun to dawn.

"What year is it?" he asked slowly.

"The year of our Lord 1706, of course," said Captain Blade. He looked hard at Sam. "Are you ailing, lad? You've gone green around the gills."

Sam had to think this out. His ancestor's letter had said the gold coin would lead him to the treasure. When he'd rubbed it he'd landed on a ship with men that talked like pirates, dressed like pirates and acted like pirates. Clearly he'd travelled back in time to a real pirate ship three hundred years in the past. No wonder they thought he was so strange!

The crew were looking at him as if they were waiting for him to do something. The letter had told him he must use his wits — that meant his brain.

"Joseph Silver, my ancestor . . ."

"Your grandfather, you mean," said Harry Hopp.

"Er . . . yes, that's right, my grandfather," said Sam quickly. After all, Joseph Silver *was* his grandfather in a way — there were just lots of 'greats' in between. "He sent me a message when he was dying." He dug in his pocket for the letter and thrust it out towards the captain. "There's a pile of gold on an island with a shark fin rock. I'm here to find it."

Captain Blade snatched the crumpled brown paper.

"What's it say, Captain?" called the crew eagerly.

"The boy's right," Blade told them. "Silver came upon a great treasure hoard."

"Well, I'll dance a jig on the bowsprit!" exclaimed a large pirate with a jolly face. "We could get more weapons if we had gold."

"True, Ned," said another. "Blackheart and his scurvy crew took nearly everything we had in that last fight."

"But we're still alive, aren't we, lads?" cried Ned, and the crew gave a ragged cheer. "Though Blackheart wants us dead and the ship sunk."

"We won't be going after this gold," announced Captain Blade firmly.

"But we always go after treasure, Captain!" exclaimed Harry Hopp as the crew shouted angrily.

Boom! Blade held a smoking gun in the air. The pirates fell silent. "Joseph Silver writes that the treasure should go to his kin and that's Sam here. We'll not go against his last wish."

"We can share the treasure," said Sam. "I'm sure that's what my . . . grandfather would have wanted."

"Don't trust him, Captain," cried Fernando.

Sam quickly showed them his coin. "Joseph Silver sent me this from the hoard."

Harry Hopp gasped. "'Tis a Double Eagle doubloon. Pure gold."

"I swear a pirate's oath on this coin," Sam said, feeling like a proper pirate. "I'm Silver's kin and I'll share his treasure with you all."

The crew cheered, huge grins splitting their grimy faces.

"Agreed," Captain Blade shook his hand. "Welcome aboard the *Sea Wolf*, Sam Silver."

"To Shark Fin Rock!" cried Sam, punching the air as the crew cheered again.

"There be only one problem," said Harry Hopp, scratching his bald head. "We've never heard of Shark Fin Rock!"

CHAPTER THREE

Sam swung himself up into the wooden crow's nest at the top of the main mast and scanned the ocean. The captain had made him lookout boy and it was an important job. He had to keep a weather eye out for their destination – the port on Tortuga Island. The captain had told him that if anyone knew about Shark Fin Rock, that was the place to find them.

But Tortuga wasn't the only thing Sam had to look out for. At any moment an enemy ship could sneak up and attack them.

The wind battered his ears and the *Sea Wolf* bucked and swayed as it ploughed through the waves, its huge sails swelling below him. This was the life for Sam. He'd been three days on a ship with a fearsome pirate crew and he didn't have to wash! That was probably because there was no one like his mum on board. No women at all, in fact. Women were bad luck and were made to walk the plank.

His mum would make *him* walk the plank if she saw the state of his clothes with three days of pirate grime all over them. He hoped she wasn't too worried about him. Perhaps he should just pop home and leave her a note to let her know he was all right.

He rubbed the coin on his sleeve, but nothing happened. He was still in the crow's nest. Sam decided he'd have a lot of

explaining to do when he finally got home.

"Sam Silver!" The first mate's voice boomed from the wheel below, making him jump. "Tortuga in view yet?"

Sam put his eye to his spyglass, the telescope that Ned the bosun had given him. "No land in sight, Mr Hopp!" he called down.

He could see the top of Harry's bald head far beneath and Fernando standing next to him, scowling up at Sam. Fernando was always scowling at him, whether he was on deck or climbing the ropes to check the rigging. Everyone had welcomed him to the crew except Fernando. He'd already knocked over the bucket when Sam was mopping the deck, broken Sam's needle when he was learning to mend a sail and complained about his snoring. Sam thought that was particularly unfair. All the crew slept below on the crowded gun deck, their hammocks side by side, and everyone snored – especially Fernando!

There was one member of the crew Sam hadn't met yet. Sinbad. And it didn't sound as if he'd be friendly, either. Captain Blade had warned him to steer clear of Sinbad. Only this morning, Ned had come to breakfast with blood on his hand.

"It was Sinbad," he'd whispered. And the rest of the crew had nodded knowingly.

Every now and then, Sam felt a prickling sensation in the back of his neck as if someone was giving him the evil eye. But when he turned there was no one there.

Sam didn't think he wanted to meet Sinbad.

He decided he had time for some sword practice. The crew had given him a few lessons and he was sure he'd soon be the greatest cutlass-wielding buccaneer that had ever lived. He didn't actually have a cutlass of his own so the spyglass would have to do.

"Have at ye, you scurvy sardine!" he yelled, lunging at the mast. The spyglass hit the wood and spun out of his hand. With horror he watched it fall, bouncing against the sails to land in a coil of rope on the deck. He had to get it back without anyone seeing. He clambered out of the crow's nest and down the rigging as fast as he could. He wished he was as fast as Fernando, who swung up and down the swaying rope ladders like a monkey.

He reached the deck and ducked down behind a cannon. Luckily everyone was too busy to notice the spyglass glinting in the sun. He crawled stealthily across the planks. He'd just reached the rope when a pair of heavy black shoes with gleaming buckles suddenly blocked his way. Slowly Sam looked up. Long coat, shiny buttons, belts full of weapons. It was Captain Blade and he didn't look happy.

"What are you doing, Sam Silver?" he demanded, rolling up the map in his hand.

"Thought I saw a rat, sir," said Sam, getting up quickly.

"Leave that to Sinbad," Captain Blade told him. "That's his job, not yours."

Sam tried to picture the bloodthirsty pirate catching a rat with his bare hands! It made him shudder.

"Back to your post, lad," the captain went on sternly. "Shout immediately you spot Tortuga."

"Aye, aye, Captain!" said Sam. He made for the rigging, retrieving the spyglass as he went.

Captain Blade strode to the stern of the

ship and climbed the steps to his cabin.

Ben Hudson, the skinny quartermaster in charge of the ship stores, was counting out coins on a barrel beside the mast. Fernando was next to him, splicing two ropes together.

Ben had a worried look on his face. "We've barely enough money to buy food," Sam heard as he got a hand on the rigging. "There'll be little left for cannonballs and gunpowder."

Fernando glared at Sam.

"*He* has a gold coin," he said. "That'll buy all we need for our treasure voyage."

"You can't have that," Sam began. "It's a very special coin . . ."

Whoosh! Fernando's dagger whistled past his ear and embedded itself in the mast. Sam hadn't even seen the boy move!

His angry shipmate stepped towards him. "Hand it over," he growled.

CHAPTER FOUR

S am stared at Fernando in horror.
"You *pretend* to be Silver's kin!"
Fernando muttered, grasping his wrist
fiercely.

"Take your hands off him." Harry Hopp
stomped up, fuming.

"He has gold," protested Fernando,
pushing Sam away. "We're a crew, we
share."

"That coin's different, lad," said Harry. "I've seen Silver's letter. The doubloon was sent to lead Sam to the treasure. It stays with him. Now get back to work. Call yourself a rigger? There's a loose pulley on the mizzenmast that needs sorting."

Fernando stormed off, cursing under his breath.

Sam was halfway up the rigging when he saw a small island on the horizon.

"Land ahoy!" he shouted. Captain Blade appeared from his cabin. "It's over there, sir. To the right."

"You mean starboard, lad," called the captain. "Remember, port's left and starboard's right." He looked through his spyglass. "That's Tortuga."

Harry Hopp bellowed instructions to the crew and at once there was a bustle of activity aboard the *Sea Wolf*.

Soon they were sailing towards the

harbour of Tortuga's one town, a noisy,
bustling place where ships of all sizes
were anchored. The ancient buildings
leaned against each other, making dark,
narrow alleyways. Houses could be seen
straggling up a steep hill and a tall
church tower rose above the shabby
roofs. It all looked like something from
a pirate film.

"Furl the sails," yelled Harry Hopp. "Drop anchor!"

Men climbed expertly along the yards to pull up the huge sails. Sam had learned that yards were the pieces of wood which stuck out from the mast and held the sails in place.

Six pirates ran to a stout metal post on the deck. They were carrying a wooden pole each, which they slotted through holes in the post. The poles stuck out like the spokes of a wheel lying on its side. The men marched round, pushing the poles and keeping the rhythm by singing a sea shanty. Slowly the chain of the heavy anchor played out from around the post and clattered over the side of the ship.

"Lower the boat," cried Captain Blade. "Harry and Ben, prepare to go ashore."

Sam scrambled down the rigging. "Can I go, too?" he asked eagerly. "It looks amazing."

"It's a rough place," said Blade. "And you're not from these parts. You wouldn't want to get lost there."

"You can't let that spy ashore, Captain," warned Fernando. "He'll lead the governor's men straight to us."

"We don't want to risk that," said Ben. "We'll be hanging from the end of a rope if the governor gets hold of us."

"I'm nothing to do with this governor, whoever he is," declared Sam hotly.

Captain Blade stroked his beard thoughtfully. Sam held his breath.

"I trust you, Sam Silver," he said, looking at him with piercing blue eyes. "You may go ashore. You will not let me down."

"Awesome!" yelled Sam, ignoring Fernando's angry glare. "I mean . . . I won't, Captain."

"But let the others ask questions about the rock," said the captain. "It has to be done secretly."

Harry Hopp tied the rowing boat to a wooden jetty.

Ben handed Sam a sleeveless jacket, a belt and a neckerchief.

"Put these on, lad," he said. "We don't want nosy folk looking at your strange clothes."

Sam followed Harry and Ben through the narrow cobbled streets. The place was full of men carrying barrels, women with baskets of fish on their heads and children whooping as they ran between them. The stench of rotting vegetables and horse dung wafted up Sam's nose.

"We're off to my cousin Barnaby's tavern," Harry called over his shoulder. "It'll be full of sailors who may know Shark Fin Rock. Then we must buy weapons and food."

Food! thought Sam. He hoped that meant the meals on board the *Sea Wolf* were going to get better. Everything Peter the cook had served up so far looked like seaweed and tasted like mud. The ship's biscuits weren't bad but you had to tap them first to get rid of the weevils or you'd be munching on a mouthful of the tiny black beetles.

Barnaby Hopp's tavern was a rough, ramshackle building. A rumble of deep voices poured from the windows. A man staggered out of the doorway, burped noisily and collapsed in a heap. They made their way past him and stepped inside. There were men everywhere, raising tankards and shouting loudly.

"Harry!" The innkeeper came forward and slapped his cousin hard on the back. He looked just like Harry Hopp except that he had a mop of curly hair. "Rums all round?" he bellowed above the noise.

"Can I have a Coke?" asked Sam.

"Who's this, talking strange?" demanded Barnaby Hopp.

"Joseph Silver's grandson," said Harry proudly. "His name's Sam. He's not from round here."

Barnaby lifted Sam off his feet in a bear hug. "Silver's kin are always welcome."

He splashed some liquid from an unlabelled bottle into four battered metal tankards.

Sam didn't understand why pirates liked rum so much. They drank it every day on the ship and he always got rid of his over the side. He thought it smelled like something his mum cleaned the chip fryer with. While the others were watching a fight in the corner, he emptied his tankard onto the floor. The rum trickled away between the rough floorboards and Sam slapped the empty tankard down on the bar.

"Well done, lad," said Harry, turning back. "You got that down you like a true pir—" He glanced around furtively. "Like a true sailor." He gestured to his cousin to come closer. "Listen, Barnaby," he said in a hoarse whisper. "Did you ever hear of a rock in the shape of a giant shark fin?"

Barnaby frowned in thought and then shook his head. "Not that I recall."

Sam's face fell. If Barnaby didn't know, who did?

"We'll ask around," Ben muttered to Harry. "But carefully. Stay there, Sam."

The two pirates sauntered around the noisy tavern, slapping men on the back and shaking hands.

"My cousin's a fine man," Barnaby told Sam. "You're lucky to sail with him and Blade."

At that moment Harry's voice could be heard above the hubbub of drinkers.

"We were blown off course and nearly

wrecked on a rock that looked like a great big shark fin," he was telling a group of buccaneers. "But I was at the wheel and I saved us. Did you ever see such a terrible rock?"

"No," came the reply. And Ben wasn't doing any better. Sam saw him catch Harry's eye and shake his head.

A thin man, his hands full of empty tankards, pushed past Sam.

"Billy forgot to take Old Abel's baccy up to him, master," he said to Barnaby, gesturing with his elbow towards a shelf.

"Sink me!" exclaimed Barnaby. "We're too busy to spare anyone now."

"Is that Abel Wagstaff you're talking about?" said Harry Hopp, coming back to join Sam. "Is that buccaneer still alive? He must be the oldest man in the Caribbean."

"Aye and still getting through a pile of tobacco each day," replied Barnaby. Then a burly sailor yelled an order and he hurried off to serve him.

Sam's brain buzzed with an idea. In his computer game, *Space Quest 3*, you had to find the oldest inhabitant of Sputnik City and ask clever questions to get information about the lost jewels of Jupiter. He could do the same here. This ancient pirate might know of Shark Fin Rock.

"How about asking Abel for information?" he whispered. "Old people have lots of memories."

"No point, lad," said Harry. "Abel once knew more about the oceans than anyone living, but these days his mind's going."

Sam suddenly thought of old Mrs Angus in Backwater Bay, who wore her shoes on the wrong feet and a sieve on her head. Everyone said her mind had gone, but she still remembered every football match she'd ever been to – and the names of the goal scorers. Maybe Abel Wagstaff was like Mrs Angus and could recall things from a long time ago. He might have the information they needed.

While Harry and Ben were discussing what to do next, Sam took the pouch of tobacco from the shelf and nipped over to Barnaby, who was heaving a drunken sailor out of the door.

"I'll take this to Abel," he offered.

Barnaby dropped the sailor in a puddle of beer and wiped his forehead with his sleeve. "That's a good deed you're doing for me, young Silver." He quickly gave Sam directions and barged his way back inside the noisy tavern.

Sam was bursting with excitement. Sam Silver, sneakiest pirate that ever lived, would get the information the crew needed and be back before they missed him. Nothing could be simpler.

CHAPTER FIVE

Sam climbed the steep cobbled street away from the tavern. Make for the church and find the door with the conch-shell knocker, that's what Barnaby had said.

The narrow road led up the hill then divided into twisting alleyways. Sam took the path to the church. He turned to stare out at the view. It was very strange

not to see any cars or telegraph poles, or
satellite dishes sticking up from
the roofs. At that moment, he felt the
strange prickling sensation on the back
of his neck that he'd felt on the ship.
He was sure he was being
watched.

He whipped round
but no one was
there. He was
relieved when he
spotted the door
with the shell
knocker. He gave
it a rap and heard
a shuffling sound as
someone moved across
the room inside.

"Ahoy there," came a cracked voice.
"State your business."

"I've got your baccy, Mr Abel, sir," Sam
called.

Bolts slid across and the door creaked open. A stooped old man in a tattered shirt and baggy breeches stood blinking in the light. He waved Sam in with a crooked hand. "Come aboard, me hearty."

He shuffled over to a battered wooden chair by a small fire. Abel's home was only one room with a barrel for a table and a bed in the corner. Sam followed him in and handed him the package of tobacco.

With shaky fingers Abel unwrapped it and filled a dirty brown pipe.

This is the perfect moment to find out about Shark Fin Rock, thought Sam.

He squatted in front of the old man. "I hear you've sailed all over the Caribbean," he said loudly.

Abel lit the tobacco and sucked hard at his pipe. "There's not a patch of these seas that I don't know."

"That's impressive!" said Sam, trying not to choke on the pipe smoke. "I've only just started being a pirate. There's a lot to learn, isn't there? For instance, when the crew had to pull on the sheets I thought it meant they had to take in the washing. I didn't know that's what the sail ropes are called."

"Takes years to learn your trade properly," said Abel, chewing on his pipe.

"And I don't know these waters very well," Sam went on. "Can you help me? I've heard of a place . . ."

But Abel wasn't listening. His eyes had misted over and he stared blankly into the distance. He had the same look as Mrs Angus in Backwater Bay when she had her sieve on.

"Hoist the topsails!" he croaked at Sam suddenly. "I'll keelhaul you, you lazy landlubber."

Sam thought he'd better do as he was told. "Aye, aye, Captain." He jumped up and pretended to pull on an imaginary rope. "Where are we heading?" he asked. "Only I've heard of this rock . . ."

Abel put down his pipe. "Take the wheel, lad," he said, heaving himself to his feet and beginning to sway as if he was on his ship.

Sam mimed turning the ship's wheel. Through the grimy little window he could see that the light was fading. Harry and Ben would be wondering where he was. With Abel's mind wandering all over the

Caribbean, it wasn't going to be as simple as he'd thought to get the information he needed.

But he had to have one more try.

"Shall I set course for the rock that's shaped like a giant shark fin, Captain?" he asked.

"What mad talk is that?" demanded the old man irritably. "There be no such place."

Sam couldn't believe his bad luck. Shark Fin Rock must be the one patch of the Caribbean that Abel had missed on his travels!

"It's really deadly," Sam said desperately, "and pointy, like the fin of a shark."

There was sudden fear in the old man's eyes as if a light had flicked on in his brain. "Arr, you don't want to go near there," he breathed. "It nearly did for me and my crew."

"Please try to remember where it is," pleaded Sam. "So that I can steer clear of it," he added quickly. "You don't want your ship to be wrecked."

Abel looked at him blankly. "What are you rambling about, boy?"

"The rock," said Sam, desperately. "You know, Shark Fin Rock."

"Don't you know where it is?"

"No!" wailed Sam. "That's why I'm asking."

The old man scratched his head. "Well, we set sail from Tortuga with the morning sun in our faces. I remember passing Gibbet Point to starboard. Then we spied a Spanish ship and went after it. It was then that we came upon the rock."

"Which way were you sailing?" urged Sam. "Which direction?"

Abel's weather-beaten forehead creased in concentration. "The sun was sinking low to port," he muttered. Sam made a mental note that that meant Abel's ship must have been travelling north.

Abel suddenly turned on Sam. "Enough of your chat, you lazy sea dog! Get back to your post this minute. We'll have no more talk of such things."

"Aye, aye, Captain," said Sam. He'd got the information he needed. He tried not to jump up and down with excitement in case Abel made him walk the plank!

The old pirate fumbled his way back to his chair, picked up his pipe and sucked loudly on the stem. He seemed to have forgotten Sam was there.

Sam silently opened the door and raced down the hill. As soon as he got back to the *Sea Wolf* with his information, they could set off for Shark Fin Rock.

The twisting alleyways were cooler now and filled with deep shadows as the sun went down. He'd noticed that it got darker much quicker in the Caribbean than in Backwater Bay. He had the sensation of being watched again. He stopped and listened for footsteps.

There were distant sounds from the harbour but up here it was eerily quiet.

He turned the corner towards Barnaby's tavern. The dark road ahead was busy with sailors pushing in and out of the door. Suddenly he heard angry cries behind him. Three men were coming down the street, their heavy boots thudding on the cobbles. They seemed to be searching for someone. The sailors saw them and shouted warnings to each other as they ran into hiding places.

"Look out!"

'It must be the governor's men!"

"Scatter!"

Sam's heart pounded. He'd be captured for sure, and he knew what happened to pirates that were taken by the governor's men.

He had to hide!

CHAPTER SIX

The shouts were coming closer. Sam looked round wildly. There was a dark passageway between two houses. He slipped into it, but now he could see it was very narrow and led to a dead end. He pushed himself against the slimy wall, hoping the shadows would hide him. At that moment he heard running footsteps and a young boy in a dirty shirt and ripped breeches appeared in the road, gasping for breath. He looked up and down, searching for some means of escape.

He must be a pirate like me, thought Sam. *I have to help him.* He gave a low whistle. The boy swung round.

"In here!" whispered Sam.

The boy darted into the passageway and squashed himself next to Sam. Sam could hear him trying to calm his frightened breathing. The men came into view and the boy fell silent, his chest heaving with the effort. One of them, a huge brute with a snarling face, stopped close by and peered intently into their hiding place. He was so close that Sam could smell his foul breath.

Sam felt the boy tense beside him. *Mustn't move a muscle,* he thought to himself. But how long could they stay like this before they were discovered? The man only had to step forward and he'd see them for sure.

"Down 'ere!" came a distant shout.

To Sam's huge relief the man swung round and thundered off along the road towards his companions.

"Thank you for not giving me away," whispered the boy. He crept along the wall towards the opening of the passageway. Sam followed. "I must leave this town while I can."

"You and me both," Sam whispered back, peering round the corner. The only light came from above, where the moon shone in the black sky. He could see the men talking together by Barnaby's tavern, which was firmly shuttered. "But we can't move yet. Those pirate hunters are still there."

The boy looked at him, puzzled. "They're not pirate hunters. They're in the pay of my horrible stepfather. They're only after me."

"So you're on the run!" said Sam, impressed. "Looks like you could do with some help."

"I would be grateful," replied the boy. "Tell me, what town is this?"

"It's the port of Tortuga, of course," said Sam. He was beginning to wonder if the boy was as mad as Abel or Mrs Angus. He wasn't sailing imaginary galleons or wearing a sieve on his head, but he was certainly different from anyone Sam had come across in the last few days. He spoke in a posh voice, which seemed very strange after all the rough pirate talk Sam had been listening to. "Where did you *think* we were?" he asked.

The boy shrugged. "I stowed away on a ship and I've been down in the hold for days. I didn't know which way we were sailing. When it docked here I jumped ashore and tried to hide, but somehow those men caught up with me."

Sam looked down the road again. The men had gone. "The coast's clear," he said. "Look, I've got to get back to my ship. My crewmates are probably waiting for me down at the harbour. Why don't you come too? I'm from the *Sea Wolf*, best pirate ship in the Caribbean. You can join us. Sounds like you'll have more chance with pirates than with your stepfather and his thugs."

"Join a pirate ship!" exclaimed the boy. "I can't do that!"

"You'd be safe if you were part of the crew," urged Sam.

The boy thought for a moment. "I can't do that — but I would be grateful for safe passage out of Tortuga."

"That's settled then," said Sam. He didn't understand why anyone would pass up the chance of being a pirate, but maybe the boy would change his mind when he saw the *Sea Wolf*. "Let's go."

Keeping their eyes and ears open, they ran down the road towards the sea. Here and there a dim light could be seen in windows but it seemed that Tortuga had shut down for the night in fear of the governor's men.

Feet slipping on the cobbles, they arrived at the end of the street that led to the harbour. Sam pulled the boy down behind a barrel while they spied out the area. In the distance, ships' lanterns could be seen, bobbing with the waves. There was no one in sight so they sped across to the harbour wall and onto the wooden jetty.

"I think we've escaped my pursuers," said the boy.

Sam's eyes swept along the jetty. There was no sign of Harry and Ben, and the boat that would take him to the *Sea Wolf* was gone.

"Looks like my crewmates have left without me!" he said, trying not to sound as worried as he felt. "We need to find a dinghy."

The boy gave him a strange look.

Perhaps they didn't use that word three hundred years ago, thought Sam. "You know," he said, "a rowing boat, to get to my ship. She's out there somewhere."

The boy nodded. He pointed along the jetty. There was a small boat moored at the very end. "What about that one? We could . . . well . . . borrow it."

"Sounds good to me," said Sam with a grin.

Keeping low, they scampered along the wooden boards towards it. Sam suddenly noticed that one of the ships in the harbour had more lanterns lit than the others. The moon came out from behind the clouds and he could make out men busy climbing the rigging to unfurl the sails. Across the water he heard the sound of the anchor chain grinding up from the seabed. A flag was being hoisted up the mainmast. As it flapped in the moonlight, Sam made out sharp teeth and a pair of crossed bones.

"That's the *Sea Wolf*," he cried. "It's sailing without us!"

CHAPTER SEVEN

The sails of the pirate ship began to fill with wind. Sam was horrified. He couldn't let the *Sea Wolf* go without them. Somehow they had to reach her.

He began to untie the rowing boat's mooring rope.

"Hey!" The shout rang in the night air. Heavy footsteps pounded towards them. It was the man who'd searched for the boy in the passageway. Sam pulled frantically at the rope, but it was too late. He felt a huge hand clamp itself to the scruff of his neck. He struggled but he was helpless. He could see the boy had been caught too, kicking desperately in the man's grasp. Now the villain had a steely arm across Sam's throat. The arm tightened and black spots danced in front of his eyes.

Suddenly an unearthly howl filled Sam's ears. A bundle of furious fur and claws flashed through the air. With a yelp of pain, the kidnapper dropped his victims and staggered away, covering his face. The yowling attacker leapt again and dug its claws into his leg.

"What was that?" gasped the boy. "Something from hell?"

"Looked like a cat!" panted Sam. "And it's saved our lives." He watched as the angry creature, hissing and spitting, drove the kidnapper back along the jetty. "I don't think it needs any help." He pulled the boy to his feet. "Let's go!"

Sam untied the boat and pushed off and they both leapt in. With an angry roar, their pursuer jumped over the hissing cat, plunged into the water and seized the stern. There were bleeding scratches on his face from the cat's attack. He reached out for the boy, making the boat rock violently.

The boy grabbed a bailing bucket and brought it down hard on the man's hands. The kidnapper cursed and fell back into the water. Sam rammed the oars into place. He was used to rowing in Backwater Bay but he'd never had to do it at night with a vicious thug after him. He pulled away with all his strength and saw the man flounder back to the jetty.

He grinned at his passenger. "Good aim with the bucket."

"He deserved it!" said the boy fiercely, fingering some bruises on his cheek.

Suddenly, there was a mewling cry and
the cat that had saved them landed in
the boat. It leapt past Sam and sat like a
figurehead on the bow, staring at the *Sea
Wolf*.

Sam wondered what the crew were going
to say when he turned up with a stray boy
and a vicious moggy.

That's if he reached the ship in time.
She was already moving slowly out of the
harbour. His shoulders were hurting but
he gritted his teeth and pulled harder.

"My name's Sam, by the way," he panted.
"I'm lookout on the *Sea Wolf*."

"I'm . . . er . . . Charlie," said the boy.

"Thank you, Sam. I thought I was going to be dragged back to my stepfather for sure."

"He sounds like a nasty piece of work," said Sam.

"He means to kill me!" declared Charlie. "But not before I've signed a will leaving all my mother's money to him. She died last year, just before my tenth birthday." Charlie looked downcast for a moment. "My stepfather told me that signing the will was just a precaution, but I know that the moment I put my name to the document I'll meet with a fatal 'accident'."

"You'll definitely be safer with the pirates," grinned Sam. He was a bit surprised to find Charlie was the same age as him. Charlie was a lot smaller.

At last, the hull of the *Sea Wolf* loomed above them. Sam caught one of the footholds that were carved into her side.

He tied the boat to a mooring ring.

"Ahoy there, *Sea Wolf!*" he yelled. "Two to come aboard." The cat turned and looked at him balefully. "I mean three!"

"Where did you get to, boy?" asked Harry Hopp as Sam hauled himself over the side rail. The first mate peered at him suspiciously in the light of his lantern. "Barnaby told us you were just delivering a pouch of baccy to Abel. It shouldn't have taken you this long. Then those men came by and we all made ourselves scarce."

"We thought you must be in the pay of the governor after all," added Ben.

Fernando rushed up and stared over the side.

"He *is* a spy I tell you!" he shouted as he spotted Charlie in the boat below. "He's brought an accomplice."

Harry shot Sam an angry glance. "Who's that?" he growled.

"We're not spies," explained Sam as the pirates began to gather round. "That's

Charlie. I was going to tell you all about him. He needs our help. I rescued him from some men who were trying to capture him because his stepfather wants to kill him and—"

"Shiver me timbers!" yelped Harry Hopp suddenly. "Sinbad's here!"

CHAPTER EIGHT

Sam spun round ready to defend himself from the terrifying pirate. But he couldn't see anyone. Sinbad must be hiding just to scare him.

There was a frantic scrabbling sound and two pointed black ears and two sets of very sharp claws appeared over the ship's rail.

"I was going to tell you all about this

moggy, too," stammered
Sam as the cat leapt onto
the deck and hissed
at everyone, its fur
bristling. "It's a bit
mangy and I'm sure
it's got fleas, but it
rescued us from those men I was telling
you about . . ."

To his surprise the crew began to chuckle.

"Well, well, well," said Harry, stamping
his wooden leg and rocking with laughter.
"So Sinbad went ashore. We thought he
was on board."

"We'd never have sailed without him if
we'd known," added Ben.

So that's *Sinbad*, thought Sam in relief.
*He's not a thug of a pirate after all, just a thug
of a cat!* And that certainly explained
why he'd kept thinking someone was
watching him. "He's very loyal to his
shipmates!" he said, backing away as the

cat suddenly flashed his claws. "In a fierce sort of way."

Harry Hopp looked down at the boat. "Come up here, lad!" he said briskly to Charlie. "Let's have a look at you."

Charlie climbed up slowly and stared defiantly at the crew.

"Doesn't look like a spy to me," said Ben. "Looks more in need of food."

"Aye," said the first mate. He turned to Fernando. "Take him below and find him some bread. Then we'll see if the captain wants him to stay. He doesn't look as if he's got the makings of a pirate."

"I don't want to be a pirate," declared Charlie, squaring his shoulders fiercely. "But if I did I'd be as good as any of you!"

"And he doesn't sound like one," said Ben. "There's not so many buccaneers from the gentry."

"Well he's very brave," said Sam. "When we stole that boat down there, a huge man tried to catch us and Charlie beat him off."

"Stole a boat from Tortuga, did you?" came Captain Blade's voice.

Sam's heart sank. Tortuga was full of pirates. Maybe the boat belonged to a rival crew who would come after the *Sea Wolf*. He'd be in dead trouble then.

Captain Blade was looking hard at him in the flickering light of the lantern. Sam gulped. Any minute now he was going to be ordered to leave the ship – or worse, made to walk the plank.

To his astonishment, Blade shook him firmly by the hand.

"Good bit of thieving, lad," he said, with a broad grin. "We'll make a pirate of you yet." He turned to Charlie, holding up the lantern and peering at the bruises on his face. "And I warrant you'll be safer with us. Now go and get fed."

Sam felt his knees go wobbly with relief. "Thank you, sir," he croaked. He waited until Charlie was out of earshot. "I've got some information. I found out which way to sail for Shark Fin Rock."

He waited to be congratulated. Instead Harry Hopp let out an oath. "The captain told you to keep your mouth shut about the treasure!" he roared. "It'll be round Tortuga before you can say swordfish."

"Don't worry, Mr Hopp," said Sam. "I never mentioned treasure."

"Harry and me couldn't find out anything," said Ben suspiciously. "Who did you hear it from?"

"Abel Wagstaff," answered Sam. "I know he's a bit confused but he remembered a rock that was shaped like a shark fin. And he said it was dangerous."

"That old seadog's lost his mind," said Harry. "You can't trust anything he says."

"Let's face it," said Ben, shaking his head. "Silver's treasure is lost to us."

"Aye," agreed Captain Blade. "We'll waste no more time on it. We have barely enough provisions to last a week, since you were scared off from getting our supplies. We're not going in circles in the hopes of stumbling upon this rock."

Sam felt like a balloon that had lost its air. Surely he hadn't been brought all this way just to watch the crew give up. He had to make them believe him.

"Hang on a sec," he burst out. "I mean, one more word with you please, Captain."

"Say your piece, lad," said Captain Blade,

"and quickly. I want you on lookout as soon as we're away from the harbour."

"I really think Abel was telling the truth," said Sam. "He said that when he saw the rock he had sailed from here with the morning sun on his face, which must mean east, and that was the same course my grandfather took."

Harry Hopp snorted in disbelief and Captain Blade shook his head.

"And then he spied Gibbet Point," Sam went on quickly. "Is that in the right direction?"

The captain and the first mate stared at him. At last Sam could see a flash of hope in their eyes.

"Stap me vitals!" exclaimed the first mate. "It is. Maybe old Abel has some sense left in him after all."

Captain Blade gave a deep, hearty laugh. "To my cabin," he ordered. "We'll cast an eye over the maps. By Neptune, we'll have this treasure yet!"

CHAPTER NINE

Captain Blade quickly lit a lantern and placed it on a table in the centre of his cabin. Then he opened a heavy wooden chest and laid out a scrolled map.

Sam looked eagerly at it. There was the Caribbean Sea, surrounded by its arc of islands. The map was hand drawn like the ones he'd seen in museums, with miniature sailing ships pictured on the sea and a cloud in the corner with a cheerful face, its cheeks full of wind.

The captain put a finger on Tortuga and traced a course due east.

"There's Gibbet Point!" Harry Hopp jabbed at a tiny island just below the words Atlantic Ocean. "Where did Abel make for after that?"

"He said he passed Gibbet Point to starboard and then sailed after a Spanish ship and the sun was sinking on the left," Sam told him. "I mean, on the port side. So that would be the west, wouldn't it?"

"Aye," said Harry. "They'd have been sailing north." He jabbed again at the map. "Round about here."

"That's uncharted sea," said the Captain solemnly. "I've heard it's deep and wild."

"That's all I know," said Sam. "But Shark Fin Rock must be somewhere near there."

Harry Hopp measured the distance with his fingers. "It's like Joseph Silver's letter said. That's two day's sail from here with a good wind."

At that moment, there was a knock on the door.

"Enter!" boomed the captain.

Ned poked his cheerful face round the door. "Waiting for your orders, Captain," he said. "Where are we heading?"

"Due east for Gibbet Point," said

Captain Blade. "I'll take the wheel now." He turned to Sam. "Get some vittles down you and then take your watch in the crow's nest."

"Aye, aye, Captain."

"And tell your new friend to report to Harry Hopp here, once he's had some food. He'll find him work."

Sam hurried off. This was his chance to see that Charlie was all right. He dashed down to the gun deck where some of the crew were taking their turn to sleep. He grabbed his small ration of bread and cheese left out on a barrel. Charlie was sitting in the corner, gnawing hungrily at his bread.

"Let's go down into the hold," whispered Sam, pointing to the stairway. "We can talk there." A small lantern hung by the hatch and he took it to light their way.

"I told you we're a good crew," said Sam as they sat on the floor of the empty hold. "You could stay, you know. We're on our way to find treasure!"

For a moment Charlie's eyes gleamed with excitement. Then he shook his head. "A pirate's life is not for me," he said. "I can't tell you why. I'll go ashore as soon as I can. There must be work for someone like me who can read and write."

"I bet you don't miss school, though," said Sam. "I don't, except for PE maybe." Charlie stared at him in puzzlement. "What's PE?"

"I mean games, athletics . . . football?" said Sam quickly. He kept forgetting how different things were three hundred years ago.

"I've heard of football," said Charlie, finishing the last crust of bread. "And I've heard grown men sometimes get killed playing it."

"Not where I come from!" exclaimed Sam. "It's the best game in the world. You'd love it." Footsteps passed over their heads. "I must get up on lookout," he told Charlie. "And the captain wants you to report to Mr Hopp. He'll give you your duties. Will you be all right? I don't reckon you're used to working."

Sam guessed that Charlie was more used to having servants. But the boy nodded his head enthusiastically.

"I'll be happy to do anything," he said. "As long as I'm free."

Two days later Sam was standing despondently in the crow's nest. It was dawn and all he could see for miles around was the sea. They'd followed Abel's route to Gibbet Point. Then changed course to sail north. That had been hours ago — and

there was still no sign of Shark Fin Rock
— or any land for that matter. The crew
were beginning to mutter that boys who
took notice of old Abel were fools.

He wished Charlie would agree to join
the crew. Perhaps he was too posh to be a
pirate. No, that couldn't be it. He didn't
mind getting dirty or working hard or
even eating Peter's cooking. And he was
certainly brave — after all, he'd run away
from his horrible stepfather. Sam couldn't
work it out, but he wished he'd change
his mind. It would be awesome to have a
friend of his own age on the crew. They'd
had great fun already. He'd taught Charlie
to play football round the deck with a
melon. In return Charlie had given him
some extra sword-fighting lessons as it
seemed that posh kids knew about that
sort of thing three hundred years ago. And
all the time Fernando had scowled at them
both and muttered under his breath.

 Sam's attention was caught by something in the distance. He checked it out through his spyglass. It was a ship, sailing across the horizon. But as he watched, the dark sails fluttered and caught the wind again. The ship was making a turn. Now she was heading straight for them. He focused on the flag that fluttered from the top of the mast. His stomach lurched. It was red with a skull that grinned evilly above a pair of crossed bones. Harry Hopp had told him about that flag. It was a flag that put terror in men's souls. It belonged to Blackheart, deadliest enemy of the *Sea Wolf*.

"Ship ahoy!" yelled Sam at the top of his voice. "Off the starboard bow. It's the *Grinning Skull!*"

CHAPTER TEN

"Hard to port!" yelled Captain Blade. "We're going to outrun them. It would be foolhardy to take them on with so few weapons."

As Sam climbed down the rigging to help, his heart hammered in his chest with fear. They were being chased by the most villainous pirate crew to sail the Caribbean. Until this adventure the scariest thing he'd ever done was to play *Attack of the Deadly Zargons* on his computer. But this was real!

"Won't they catch up with us?" he asked the captain.

"No lad," said Blade. "We're lighter and faster. We'll be away once we've changed course." He turned an excited face to Sam. "Blackheart's not going to see the colour of our innards this time."

"I'd be ready if he did, sir!" said Sam, trying to be as brave as the captain.

"Then you're a credit to your grandfather!" replied Blade.

Sam ran to help the crew pull on the sheets and bring the sails round. Charlie came over and took the end of the rope behind him. Sam gave him a grin.

"You'll be turning into a pirate before you know it," he said.

"I'm not joining your crew," panted Charlie. "But it looks like you lily-livered lot need my help!"

The *Sea Wolf* began to turn but it was taking too long. The *Grinning Skull* was bearing down on them and ripples of fear were running through the crew.

BOOM! The sound of the enemy cannon made Sam feel as if all his teeth had come loose in his head. It was even louder than the time the oven had exploded at home and they'd had to call the fire brigade.

Cannonballs pounded into the water, making the ship rock with each blast. A missile whizzed over their heads and smashed into one of the top sails. The sail was ripped from its tethers and flapped uselessly.

"Get that repaired!" ordered the captain. "We need all the sail we can muster."

Sam saw Fernando swing up the rigging and sit astride the end of the top yard, trying to secure the hanging sail. There was another deafening blast from the enemy ship. A cannonball flew past Fernando and hit the yard he was sitting on. It almost snapped in two. Fernando gave a cry as he lost his balance. Arms flailing, he caught hold of the broken yard with one hand.

Sam watched in horror. Fernando was hanging helplessly, high over the deck. It didn't matter that he hated Sam. He was Sam's shipmate and Sam had to help him before he fell to his death. As the cannonballs flew all around, he pulled himself up the mast and leaned out to grasp Fernando's wrist. But he was too far away.

He edged out on to the broken yard and tried again. But even now his fingertips could only just touch Fernando's hand. He needed to get further out.

Creak! The end of the yard was threatening to snap. There wasn't much time.

Sam hooked his legs through the rigging and stretched out on his stomach along the wooden spar. He could see Fernando's wild eyes looking up at him. He made a

grab for Fernando just as the yard broke
and tumbled to the deck.

"Got you!" he cried, seizing his
shipmate's wrist and feeling Fernando's
full weight almost dragging him off the
spar. Sam strained every muscle to try and
pull his shipmate up, but it was hopeless.
Suddenly Fernando began to swing
backwards and forwards.

"What are you doing?" cried Sam.
"We'll both fall!"

"Trust me!" panted Fernando. He swung
his legs higher and higher, then, just when
Sam thought he couldn't hold on any
longer, Fernando hooked one foot over
the yard and, with a quick twist, heaved
himself up until he was sitting next to Sam.

"Thank you," he said awkwardly. "You're
a true shipmate. I should never have
doubted you."

"It was teamwork," answered Sam,
checking that his arm hadn't dropped off.

"We were stuck until you flipped yourself on to the yard. You should be a trapeze artist!"

Fernando looked at him. "What strange talk is that? You may have saved my life but you're still mad! Now let's get off this yard before the rest of it breaks."

As they climbed down the rigging, Sam realised he hadn't heard a cannonball whiz past his ears for a while.

"Look what's happening," he called to Fernando. "We're winning the race."

The *Grinning Skull* was behind them now. The *Sea Wolf* had made her turn and was starting to pull away.

Grim-faced pirates stood at the rails of the enemy ship, cursing and shaking their fists. Amongst them stood a huge, terrifying figure, urging them on with his sword. He wore a long, flowing black coat and a massive three-cornered hat. Sam quickly took in his wild grey hair and beard, heavy gold earrings and the eye patch over his left eye. This must be Blackheart. And he didn't look happy.

Captain Blade leapt up onto the poop deck, his coat tails flying. "Well done, men," he cried. "We've outwitted them."

But Sam could see Blackheart reaching into his belt. Slowly he raised a large pistol and aimed it at Blade's head.

There was a cry from the rigging and a small figure suddenly swung across on a rope. It was Charlie! As Blackheart fired, the boy thudded into Blade and sent him sprawling on to the deck. The bullet smashed into the mizzen mast where the captain had been standing a second before.

"Go, Charlie!" breathed Sam.

Fernando gave him a nudge. "So we have two trapeze artists on the *Sea Wolf*."

Blackheart struggled to reload but as he tried to take aim again he seemed to realise it was no good. The *Sea Wolf* was rapidly moving out of range.

"This isn't over, Blade," he bellowed. "I rule these seas and I'll destroy you."

"But not today!" replied Captain Blade, rising and giving him a sweeping bow.

Sam caught the rage on Blackheart's face and then the *Grinning Skull* was left behind.

"Get back on a north heading, Mr Hopp," ordered the captain. He turned to Charlie and helped him to his feet. "Thank you, lad. I owe you my life."

Charlie stood to attention. "Just doing my duty, Captain," he said.

Sam's hopes rose. Maybe Charlie had

changed his mind about joining the crew.

Captain Blade looked up at the sky. The early morning sun was rising over the bow. "I said north, Mr Hopp. Why are we going east?"

"I can't change course, Captain!" The first mate yelled from the wheel, his knuckles white as he tried to turn the ship. "We must be caught in a current!"

The *Sea Wolf* was swaying helplessly from side to side as if it was being pulled by invisible ropes. The crew shouted to each other in fear as they struggled with the sail sheets. Sam and Fernando raced to help but nothing worked.

"Rocks ahead!" came a terrified cry.

Sam looked up and the blood froze in his veins. A line of towering peaks rose in their path, the waves sucking and crashing at their base.

The *Sea Wolf* was going to be smashed to pieces.

CHAPTER ELEVEN

"Pull hard on those sheets, men," ordered Captain Blade, striding over to Harry Hopp to give him the extra strength needed to move the wheel. "We'll turn this ship if it's the last thing we do. Sam, get up aloft and tell us what you see."

Sam scrambled up the rigging and pulled himself into the crow's nest.

He wiped the salt spray from his eyes

and looked at the crashing waves ahead. He could hear the cries of the men straining at the sails. But no matter what they did the *Sea Wolf* ploughed on towards the rocks.

Sam suddenly found the gold coin in his clenched fist. How had that got there? Was it telling him to get out of danger and go back to his own time before it was too late?

"No!" Sam shouted to the wind. He was a Silver, and a Silver would never abandon his crew no matter what the danger.

The coin tingled and grew warm in his hand. Now he seemed to hear a deep voice. "Head for Shark Fin Rock."

He looked round wildly. Shark Fin Rock couldn't be in these waters. It had to be near an island and Sam saw no sign of an island here. But out of nowhere a huge point suddenly loomed above the rest, black against the sky. It was the shape of an enormous shark's fin. It must be the rock they'd been looking for. The rock that had nearly wrecked Old Abel's ship and had done for Joseph Silver.

But why was the coin telling him to head for it? Surely that way was death to any vessel! Then he remembered Silver's letter. The coin would lead him to the treasure. Sam had to trust what it told him.

"Head for the biggest rock!" he yelled at the top of his voice. "Full speed ahead."

"Have you lost your wits, boy?" called Harry Hopp angrily.

"No, Mr Hopp," shouted Sam in desperation. "I'm *using* my wits – just like Silver's letter said. We have to do this! That's Shark Fin Rock."

"How dare you tell me—" began Harry.

"Harry!" snapped Captain Blade as the first mate fought to turn the wheel against the raging sea. "We'll do as the boy says."

"But Captain—" protested Harry fearfully.

"It's our only hope." The Captain was deadly serious.

The ship lurched towards the rock, bucking dangerously in the waves that smashed hard against the bows.

And then Sam saw it — a gap in the rocks. It had been hidden by the shark's fin. It looked impossibly narrow but it was their only chance.

"To starboard!" he yelled, pointing frantically. "Now!" He held his breath.

Could they make it in time? The sails cracked as the crew fought the wind. He felt the ship lurch to the right, the timbers creaking in protest. He closed his eyes, waiting for the sound of wood smashing on hard rock . . . but it didn't come.

Sam opened his eyes. He could not believe the sight in front of him. The *Sea Wolf* was sailing calmly into a tiny hidden bay. The sea sparkled in bright sunlight and waves lapped on golden sands. Tall trees covered the hilly slopes of the island and he could see rocks and caves just waiting to be explored.

The crew sent up a loud cheer.

Sam jumped down onto the deck and high fived with the mast in his excitement. They'd reached the island they'd been searching for. Now the treasure must be within their grasp.

Soon the anchor was dropped and the crew were pouring out of the rowing boats and onto the beach. Sam looked all round. It was amazing to think that behind such vicious rocks lay this amazing island full of treasure.

"Well, swing me on the anchor!" Ned had a beaming smile on his round face. "You got us here, Sam!"

Harry Hopp held up a bottle of rum. "To young Silver!" he declared as he took a swig and passed it round. "You've got your grandfather's skill and no mistake."

The crew cheered and Fernando slapped Sam on the shoulder.

"I am sorry for ever thinking you were a spy," he said. "You are a true friend."

"I couldn't have done it without all of you!" said Sam in delight. This was better than the time he'd scored the winning goal in the school challenge cup.

"You're a credit to the *Sea Wolf*," Captain Blade told him. "Now, before we get searching for that treasure, there's something else I have to do. Step forward, Charlie. I want you to join the crew and I won't take no for an answer."

Sam looked round for his friend. How could Charlie refuse now? But he couldn't see him anywhere. Then someone burst from the back of the crowd and dashed away across the sand, making for the trees beyond.

"Charlie!" Sam yelled. "Come back."

But his friend didn't stop, so Sam set off after him. He remembered that Charlie had said he couldn't join the crew. Was that why he was running? Sam had to find out.

He caught up just as Charlie was slipping out of sight into a small cave. Sam rugby-tackled him to the ground.

"Let me go," panted Charlie desperately. "I must get away."

"But we need you," Sam told him. "And

anyway, you can't stay here. This is just an island. There's no one around to help you. You'll never survive on your own."

"You don't understand . . ." began Charlie.

"You can't go against the captain," said Sam. "He wants to welcome you to the crew."

"He won't when he finds out," muttered Charlie, shaking sand out of his shirt.

"Finds out what?" Sam jumped up and looked at him in alarm. "You're not a spy, are you?"

Charlie shook his head, looking grim. "It's worse than that. I'm a girl."

Sam burst out laughing.

"What's so funny?" said Charlie indignantly. "My real name is Charlotte Fleetwood.

I only dressed like this as a disguise when I escaped."

"I don't see the problem," said Sam. "Girls are as good as boys any day."

But Charlie was gazing fearfully at the crew who were all looking their way. "Pirates won't have girls on board their ships. Even I know that. They say it's bad luck."

Sam's face fell. He'd forgotten that. The pirates were always going on about their superstitions and the terrible things that would happen if they didn't put their left shoe on first or touch the main mast every time they saw a purple-billed seagull. And the thought of having a female on board made them shake in their breeches. Then it came to him. They didn't have to know.

"You'll just have to keep your disguise, then," he said with a grin. "After all, you've got away with it so far."

Charlie thought about this for a moment. "I'd like nothing better than to join the crew . . ."

"It's sorted then," said Sam. "I won't give you away."

"You promise?"

Sam put his hand on his heart. "I swear a pirate oath," he said solemnly. "Come on. I'll take you back to the captain."

He held out a hand. Charlie grasped it and leapt to her feet. A horrified look came over her face.

"What's the matter?" asked Sam.

"I can feel something under my foot," she said in a small voice. "It's thin and hard and it snapped as I stood up."

Gingerly she stepped aside.

Sam knelt and brushed the sand away. To his amazement, he found himself staring at a finger bone!

Cautiously, he uncovered more bones, working his way up the arm to a shoulder blade and finally to a human skull, its jaw lolling open in a grotesque smile.

"It's a skeleton!" Sam whispered.

CHAPTER TWELVE

Sam and Charlie gazed in silence at the
skeleton.

Something was glinting in the sunshine.
Sam rummaged in the sand beside the
bones and pulled out a tattered belt with a
tarnished buckle.

He peered at it closely. The buckle was
engraved with an image. "It's a wolf's
head, just like the one on the flag. This

was Joseph Silver!"

They stood up. Sam felt strangely sad to see the remains of his ancestor. It was as if the island had taken care of the burial. Birds must have picked his bones clean and the wind had covered him with sand.

There was something odd about the way the skeleton was lying. It was curled on its side but one arm was straight, with a single finger pointing towards the small dark cave.

"He's showing us where the treasure's hidden," said Sam. "He was a true pirate to the end!"

"Ahoy there!" he yelled to the crew. "We've found something."

Sam and Charlie led the way to the cave, the crew surging after them with excited shouts.

Captain Blade took Charlie firmly by the arm. "I hope you weren't trying to desert, young man," he said, pretending to look stern.

"Of course not, sir," replied Charlie with a twinkle in her eye. "I was just trying to find the treasure and save you the trouble."

The captain gave a hearty laugh. "Then you can go with Sam and be the first to set eyes on it. Fernando, Harry and Ben, follow with me. The rest of you give Joseph Silver a decent burial."

Harry Hopp lit a flaming torch and held it high as Sam and Charlie stooped to enter the cool shadows. Sam's eyes swept round the craggy grey walls for signs of the treasure. The cave was empty, but at the far end a narrow tunnel stretched away into the dark.

"Through there!" Ducking and twisting, Sam led them along the passageway. The shadows from Harry's torch rippled across the walls, showing the tunnel leading down into the earth. Sam could hear the others behind, swearing as they grazed themselves on the jagged walls. He checked each crevice and hollow in the rocks, but nothing glinted in the torch flame. At last the tunnel opened out into a large underground cavern, where their voices echoed eerily.

"Now what?" asked Harry. "I see no treasure here."

"But it must be!" insisted Sam, looking wildly round.

"It's possible someone got here before us," said Captain Blade, putting a hand on Sam's shoulder.

"They can't have, Captain," answered Sam firmly. "We must keep looking." Surely he would not have been guided all this way and through so many dangers if the hoard had already been taken.

Charlie was feeling along the walls of the cavern. "There's a hole here!" she called suddenly. "I can just get my arm in. And I can feel something inside."

Sam joined her and soon the two of them had pulled away enough loose stones and rock to show a small, dark chamber beyond. The light from Harry's torch fell on a pile of wooden caskets. The nearest one was open, and a pile of golden goblets glinted in the light.

"It's the treasure!" Sam gasped, hardly able to believe his eyes. "I knew it would be here!"

"By thunder!" exclaimed Blade, taking his turn to look. "That's a fine hoard."

Ben ran his hands around the opening. "It's solid rock," he said. "And that hole's too small for us to pass through."

"Not for me, it isn't," said Sam. "Permission to enter the treasure cavern, Captain!"

Captain Blade nodded. Sam wriggled through the gap. Harry lit another torch and handed it through the hole.

Sam held the light over the treasure. Whoever had put it there had found a great hiding place. There was only the one little entrance, and they'd been lucky to find that. The bumpy floor was covered in solid wooden caskets. Sam lifted each lid in turn, mesmerised by the sight of so many jewels and coins. But he knew he mustn't waste time. He wedged the torch between some rocks and tried to heave one of the caskets up through the hole.

"It's too heavy for me to lift," he called.

"Then hand it out bit by bit," shouted Harry Hopp impatiently.

As Sam began to pass out the necklaces and gold rings, chains and diamond-encrusted brooches, he realised he could hear faint cracking, grinding noises, as if the rocks were shifting above his head. He doubled his speed. He had just thrown out the last bag of coins when there was a loud rumble and a crack like thunder, and rocks and stones suddenly crashed down in front of him. The torch went out and he was plunged into darkness.

Sam's heart beat wildly as he tried to feel his way out of the cave. But his fingers touched solid rock. His only exit had gone.

He listened for sounds of the crew trying to rescue him, but there was a deep, dead silence. He shouted, but no one answered.

A terrible idea began to grow in Sam's mind.

Now that the crew had got the treasure, they didn't need him any more. Had they taken their riches and left him here to die?

CHAPTER THIRTEEN

Sam's fingers scrabbled away at the loose earth and rocks. He wasn't a Silver for nothing. He'd dig himself out. This island had done for his ancestor, but it wasn't going to do for him too!

"I'll show those pirates they can't leave me here," he muttered as he dug for his life.

He heard the sound of rock scraping on

rock. Soil and stones fell all around him. He'd started another landfall! He covered his head.

Something burst through the loose earth and grasped him round the wrist. He peered down, realising that a faint light was now shining in. He saw a strong hand wearing a ring with a blood red stone set into it.

"Look lively, lad!" Captain Blade's voice echoed round the chamber. "We can't hang around in here all day. We've got treasure to load."

In seconds Sam was pulled free. At that moment there was a terrible rumbling noise overhead.

"Run!" yelled Harry Hopp. "The whole thing's coming down."

They'd just reached the mouth of the cave when there was a boom inside the cliff. They threw themselves onto the sand as choking dust and debris burst over

them. When Sam looked back, the cave
had disappeared.

It was a very cheerful crew who stacked
up the treasure on the beach. The *Sea Wolf*
sat at anchor in the quiet waters of the bay
and the sun shone down from a blue sky.

"This is a good island," said Captain
Blade, gazing at the golden sand and lush
forest. "Plenty of fruit and the bay's full
of fish."

"Aye," said Harry Hopp, mopping his brow. "There be gallons of fresh river water too."

Sam looked up from the doubloons he was counting. "This island would make a great hideout," he said.

"Good idea, my friend," answered Fernando. "No one else knows there's a bay here and it's well protected by Shark Fin Rock. We could come here between voyages to rest and store our treasure."

"I can think of nowhere better," said Captain Blade. "And as it doesn't appear on any map you can have the honour of naming it, Sam."

"I've got the perfect pirate name," said Sam. "Skeleton Island."

"Excellent," agreed Captain Blade. "Skeleton Island it is. Ned, we need to build a stronghold with a stockade around to protect it. We'll find a good spot deep in the forest."

"Aye, aye, Captain," said Ned cheerily, calling to Fernando and some of the men to gather tools. "There's plenty of wood here for that."

"Harry, you take a party back to the ship to store some of this gold," the captain went on. "We'll leave the rest in the hideout."

Sam and Charlie helped Harry and his team load the booty into one of the rowing boats and soon they were back on the *Sea Wolf*.

"It'll be good to have a full hold again," said Ben, handing a pile of heavy gold plates to Charlie. "Stash these safely, lad."

"You're a fine worker, Charlie," said Harry Hopp, as he climbed over the rail, sacks of doubloons on his shoulder. "I mean, for someone who's known luxury. Who was this terrible stepfather that made you leave such a comfortable life?"

"Eustace Gilbert . . ." Charlie began.

Harry's eyes narrowed. "Great guns!" he roared. "You did well to leave that scoundrel's house. He's more of a villain than Blackheart!"

Ben nodded vigorously. "There's no honour in that hornswaggler. He's a cheat and a liar."

"Wait a minute." Harry Hopp was staring at Charlie suspiciously. "I heard he married a widow."

"That was my mother," said Charlie.

"A widow with money . . . and one child." Harry's voice was harsh. "A daughter." He pushed his stubbly face into Charlie's.

"Stop that," shouted Sam, trying to pull Harry away.

The first mate shoved him aside and grabbed Charlie's arm. "Shiver me timbers, we've got a girl aboard!"

"What are you talking about?" blustered Sam. "I can't see a girl here."

"I won't have you lying on my behalf, Sam," said Charlie quietly. "Yes, I am a girl. My name's Charlotte Fleetwood."

The nearby crew members began to mutter angrily. Sam rounded on them.

"It shouldn't matter that she's a girl," he said desperately. "We've seen how hard she's worked on the *Sea Wolf*. If we don't help her we're as bad as her stepfather."

"Females are bad luck!" snapped Harry Hopp.

"But she's been *good* luck," insisted Sam. "She saved the captain's life."

"I bet we'd never have had that encounter with Blackheart if she hadn't been aboard to curse us," shouted Peter the cook.

"That was the bad luck working, right enough," called someone nervously.

"And if we keep her there'll be more," came another voice.

Harry Hopp stamped his wooden leg.

The crew fell silent. "There's only one thing for it," he snarled. "She'll have to walk the plank."

To Sam's horror there was a chorus of "Aye, fetch the plank" and a length of timber was thrust over the side. Harry Hopp pushed Charlie up onto it and turned her towards the sea.

"No!" cried Sam, trying to pull her back. Two crew members grabbed him and held him fast. "You can't allow this."

"It's what the crew wants," said Harry Hopp. "Isn't that right, men?"

The shouts of "Aye" came out in a deafening roar.

"Don't fret, Sam," said Ben. "It's calm water here. She can swim to shore."

"But she'll be left on the island on her own when we go!" protested Sam, horrified. "Can't we at least take her to the next port?"

"A woman on board has to walk the

plank," said Harry Hopp roughly. "It's our way." He pulled out his cutlass and pushed the point into Charlie's back. "Walk!" he commanded.

With faltering steps, Charlie edged along the plank. It wobbled as she neared the end. She tried to look back at Sam but Harry Hopp waved the blade at her.

"Go on!" he growled. "You'll easily make it to shore. It's not like you're going to drown. Jump!"

Other crew members took up the word, muttering it under their breath. "Jump, jump, jump."

Charlie looked down at the deep water of the bay.

"I *will* drown, Mr Hopp," she said in a small voice. "I can't swim."

Chapter Fourteen

Sam struggled to break free.

"Let me jump, too," he shouted. "I can help her."

"You stay out of this . . ." Harry Hopp began.

But suddenly a streak of black fur shot out from under the nearest cannon and landed with a thump on the plank.

"Sinbad's come to see her off!" called a

gleeful voice from the back.

The ship's cat hissed and spat at the crew then, tail in the air, stalked along towards the shivering girl. Charlie bent down to stroke him.

"Watch out!" cried Sam. "He'll scratch you! He's vicious . . ."

He broke off. Sinbad was nudging Charlie's legs with his head. She picked him up and he settled in her arms like a baby. His purrs could be heard all over the deck.

"You'd better take him," said Charlie, offering him to Harry Hopp. "I don't want him to go overboard with me."

Harry Hopp backed away. The black cat flexed his claws and glared balefully at him.

"I've been thinking," Ben started. "If Sinbad reckons she's all right . . ."

"We'll all feel his claws if we hurt a friend of his," muttered Peter the cook.

"What do we do now, Harry?" whispered Ben.

"Charlie can stay on board," said the first mate decisively. "I'm sure the captain will agree. She may be a girl, and *usually* that's bad luck, but it'll be even worse luck if we go against Sinbad."

"True enough!" said Peter, nodding with relief.

"Sinbad always has good sense," agreed Ben as Charlie jumped down and the plank was stowed away. "But who's going to tell the captain we've got a female on board?"

"What's this?" demanded a stern voice and Captain Blade swung over the rail.

Sam gulped. "Charlie's really a girl," he gabbled, "but she's not bad luck because Sinbad likes her so can she stay?"

The captain looked in astonishment at Charlie, who was still cradling Sinbad in her arms.

"By the heavens!" he exclaimed. "Anyone who can save the captain's life *and* tame

that wild beast certainly deserves to be a member of this crew, female or not."

Merow!

Sinbad swiped at the captain. Then he sprang out of Charlie's arms, sharpened his claws on Harry Hopp's wooden leg and disappeared down onto the gun deck.

"That's settled then," said Captain Blade, mopping his brow on his sleeve. "Now, let's get ready to sail for Tortuga! We've got money to spend."

Sam scanned the horizon from his perch in the crow's nest. This was the life, a happy pirate crew and a ship bursting with treasure. They were heading back to Tortuga and this time they were going to buy all the supplies they needed – and more. He couldn't wait to see what happened next . . .

But all at once Sam felt a strange tingling in his fingers and toes. The line between the sea and sky began to spin and he was sucked inside a dark churning tunnel. He closed his eyes.

Thump! He landed on a floor. He felt about with his hands. He was on a soft carpet. He opened his eyes. His jerkin, belt, neckerchief and spyglass had vanished and he was back in his bedroom above the fish and chip shop!

"Sam!" It was his mum. How was he going to explain where he'd been for the last few days? "Hurry up! I told you I need you on the till – now."

Sam couldn't believe it. He'd been back to the past, joined a pirate crew, rescued a runaway, escaped the deadly band of the *Grinning Skull* and found treasure. But here in Backwater Bay it seemed no time had passed at all. Awesome!

"Coming, Mum!" he yelled.

He slipped the gold doubloon inside its bottle. He needed to keep it safe so that he could join the crew of the *Sea Wolf* again. But he also needed to keep his time-travelling adventures a secret. He wasn't sure his mum would approve of pirate battles and dangerous sea voyages! Sam grinned to himself as he put the bottle safely back on its shelf. Nobody in *his* world could ever know, but Sam Silver, Undercover Pirate, would be ready for his next adventure . . .

The Sea Wolf

Charlie Fleetwood
Deckhand

Ben Hudson
Quartermaster

Sam Silver
Lookout

Ned Wainwright
Bosun

Harry Hopp
First Mate

CREW MANIFEST

Sinbad

Thomas Blade
Captain

Peter Craddock
Ship's Cook

Fernando
Rigger

Don't miss the next exciting adventure in the
Sam Silver: Undercover Pirate series

THE GHOST SHIP

Available now!
Read on for a special preview
of the first chapter.

CHAPTER ONE

It was a rainy Monday morning and Sam Silver was getting ready for school. But he wasn't happy about it.

"I can't believe Mr Nodsworthy has banned football for a whole week," he grumbled to himself. "Just because someone booted the ball and flattened Class Four's tomatoes."

Then an idea shot into his head like

a cannonball. He knew how to cheer himself up. He snatched an old bottle from his shelf and shook out an ancient gold doubloon.

Sam was always finding interesting objects on the beach at his home in Backwater Bay but this sand-pitted bottle was extra special. Not only had he found a gold coin inside but he'd also discovered a letter from an ancestor of his, a fierce pirate called Joseph Silver. The letter had told him where a great hoard of treasure lay and when he'd rubbed the coin an amazing thing had happened. He'd been whisked back more than three hundred years to 1706 and joined the crew of a really cool pirate ship, the *Sea Wolf*! Captain Blade and his brave men liked nothing better than sailing the Caribbean to find treasure, so they'd all set off straight away.

Sam decided to see what the pirates were up to right now. And he didn't have to worry that his mum and dad would miss him and start sending out search parties — not one second passed in the present while he was being a buccaneer.

Sam quickly changed out of his school uniform into the tatty jeans and T-shirt he'd worn on the *Sea Wolf*. He didn't dare risk getting his uniform all ripped and torn! His mum would go mad.

He rubbed the coin on his sleeve and waited for the dizzy feeling he'd felt last time he'd been whisked away into the past. Nothing happened. He rubbed it harder but still found himself sitting on his bed. Sam stared miserably at the doubloon. Perhaps it only worked once and he'd never find himself on board the *Sea Wolf* ever again. His heart sank to his trainers.

Then he remembered — last time he'd spat on the coin before he rubbed it. Perhaps he needed Silver spit to make it work. He decided to give it a try . . .

All around him Sam's bedroom walls set off in a fast spin. There was a deafening rush of air and he had the feeling he was being sucked into a giant vacuum cleaner. He closed his eyes in delight.

"*Sea Wolf*, here I come!" he shouted.

Sam landed with a thud on a hard wooden floor and opened his eyes.

Awesome! He was in the storeroom on board the pirate ship just like last time.

But before he could move, his ears were split by the loudest scream he'd ever heard.

A girl with roughly chopped hair and pirate breeches was standing over him, shrieking at the top of her voice.

It was his friend Charlie. Sam staggered to his feet. She must have seen him pop up out of nowhere. How was he going to explain that?

Charlie grabbed a mop. "The ghost of

Sam Silver!" she yelled, trying to whack him over the head with it. "Come back to haunt us! Get away from me, you horrible spook!"

"I'm not a ghost," said Sam, dodging the wet mop head.

"Oh, yes you are," said Charlie, waving it in his face. "When you disappeared in the middle of the ocean the crew said you must have drowned. And now a week later you appear out of thin air! No mortal being can do that. Be gone, you fiend from hell!"

"You've got it wrong—" Sam began.

"I thought you were my friend," Charlie went on crossly, chasing him round the storeroom. "Friends don't come back and scare each other when they're dead."

The wet mop slapped down on his head.

"Yuck!" cried Sam, wiping his eyes. "Look, if I was a ghost that would have gone straight through me, wouldn't it?"

Charlie looked at the water dripping off Sam's nose. "I suppose so," she said doubtfully.

"I really am alive," insisted Sam.

"Ahoy there, Charlie," came a shout from the deck above, "are you all right?"

For a moment it looked as if Charlie was going to call for help.

"You must believe me," Sam pleaded.

"Charlie!" came the shout again. "What be the matter?"

"All's well," Charlie called back. "I'll be up soon." She put down the mop. "You've got some explaining to do, Sam Silver," she said. "One minute I'm in here looking for sail thread and the next minute you appear at my feet with a stupid grin on your face."

Sam took a deep breath. There was only one thing for it. He had to tell her the truth.

He peered out of the storeroom door to make sure no one was within earshot. "You know how I sometimes say things that are a bit strange."

Charlie nodded. "Like com-put-ers . . . and . . . phones . . . and girls playing football?"

Sam nodded. "You see, I don't come from your time. I'm from the twenty-first century." Charlie's eyes grew wide with amazement and her mouth dropped open as he told her how the coin brought him to the *Sea Wolf*. "That's why I appeared from nowhere," he finished.

"You're talking like a mad man," said Charlie, waving the mop again.

Sam took out his coin. "I swear a pirate's oath on Silver's doubloon that I am a time traveller."

Charlie looked thoughtful.

"You know you can trust me," Sam insisted. "I helped you escape from your stepfather's men, didn't I?"

"Well, yes . . ." Charlie admitted.

"And I didn't tell the crew that you were really a girl, did I?"

"No."

"And when they found out and said females were bad luck on board," Sam went on, "I tried to stop them making you walk the plank."

"That's true," said Charlie slowly.

"Then you have to believe this," pleaded Sam. "But don't tell anyone, not even Fernando."

Charlie put down her mop. "Very well."
She grinned. "Your secret's safe with me.
The crew would think *I* was mad if I told
them the tale you've just told me."

Sam held up his hand. "High five!"
Charlie looked puzzled. "It's what we do
in the future when we're happy. You slap
my hand with yours."

Charlie smacked her palm onto his.
"The men will be delighted to find that
you're alive!" she exclaimed.

"There's only one problem," said Sam.
"How am I going to explain where I've
been?"